ABCs

of

NEW

HAMPSHIRE

ABCs

of

NEW

HAMPSHIRE

HARRY W. SMITH

DOWN EAST BOOKS

Dedicated
to
everyone who loves
NEW HAMPSHIRE

A
Ambling Androscoggin

B

Bear in
Birches

C

Carefree Canoeing

D

Dependable Dogs

E

Efficient
Engine

F

Flitty
Finches

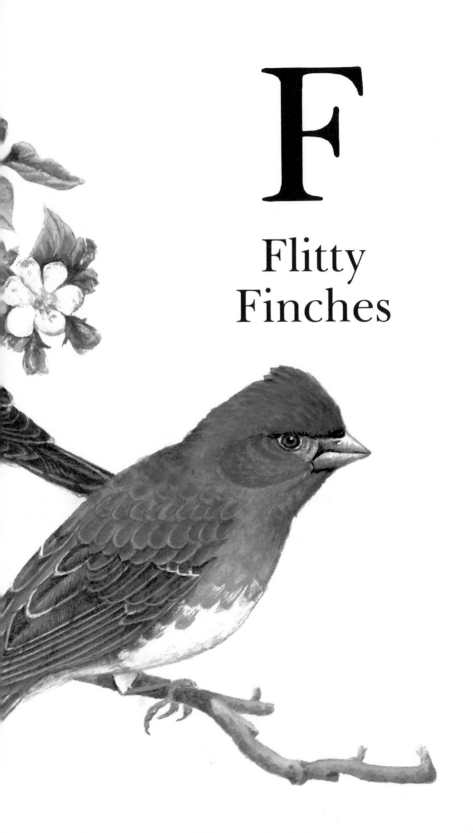

G

Grey
Granite

H

Hatchery
Helper

I
Intriguing
Isles

J
Jay in Juniper

K

Kitten in Knapsack

L
Lavender
Lilacs

M
Man of the
Mountain

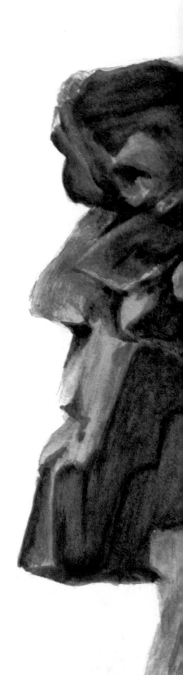

N

Natural
Notch

O

Observant
Owls

P

Port of
Portsmouth

Q
Quilting a
Quilt

R

Rascal
Raccoons

S

Sandy
Seashore

T

Tempted
Trout

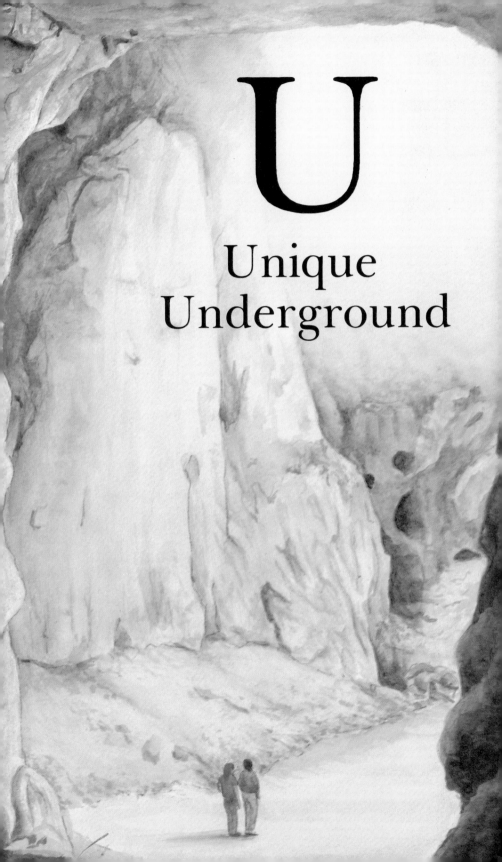

U

Unique
Underground

V

Valley
Vista

W

Windy
Washington

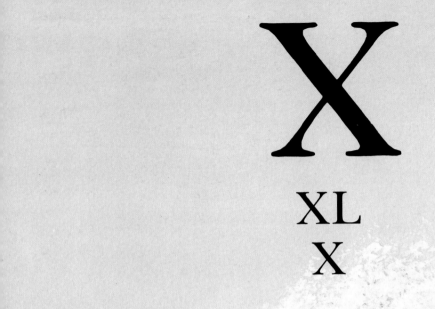

X

XL
X

Y

Yankee
Youth

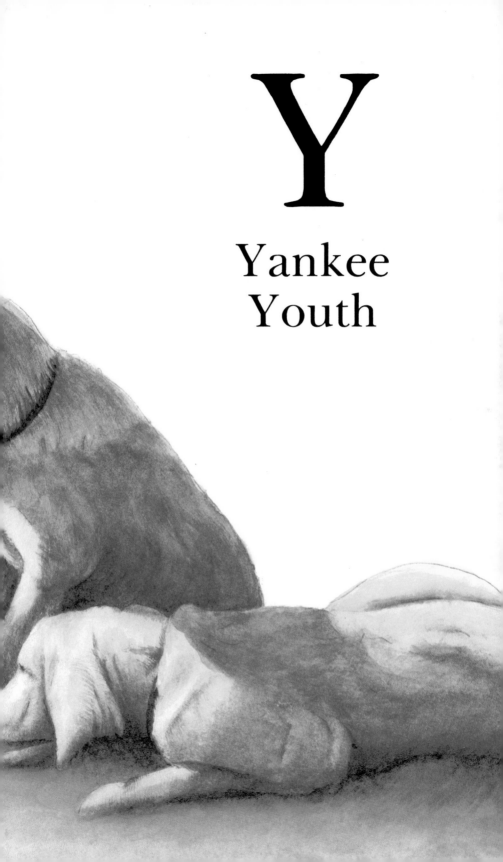

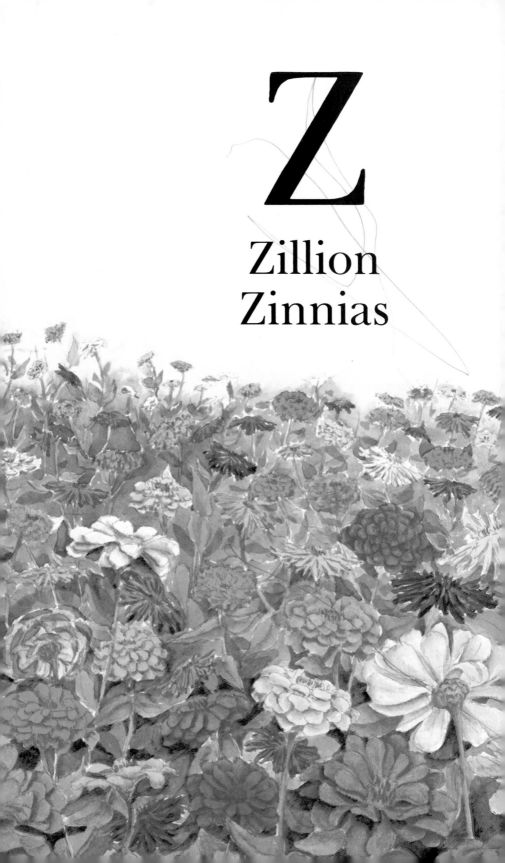

Z
Zillion
Zinnias

A   The Androscoggin River begins in northeastern New Hampshire and flows south to Gorham, then east into Maine.

B   Black bears still roam the remote mountain forests of New Hampshire. Bears usually hunt alone, searching for berries, nuts, insects, small animals, and honey. The white birch is the state tree of New Hampshire.

C   New Hampshire's many beautiful lakes and rivers make the state ideal for canoeists.

D   Dogsleds are an old method of winter transportation. Today the sled dogs are used more for fun and races than out of necessity. Siberian huskies and Alaskan malamutes are the most common breeds used to pull the sled and "musher," or sled driver, across the snow.

E   The cog railroad that runs up the western slope of Mount Washington is 3½ miles long, with grades as steep as 37 percent. Special steam locomotives were built to climb the steep mountainside. The engines have heavy, toothed wheels that notch securely into the cog rails. The boiler is lower in front so that it will be level as the engine moves up the slope.

F   The purple finch is New Hampshire's state bird. It is about the size of a sparrow and is the color of red raspberries.

G   New Hampshire is called the Granite State. Thousands of years ago huge glaciers carved the state's mountains, valleys, and gorges out of the solid granite bedrock.

H   Game fish such as bass, trout, and salmon are raised in fish hatcheries. When the fish reach the proper size, they are removed from the large tanks in which they are grown and released in many of the state's lakes and streams.

I The Isles of Shoals, so named because of the fish that school, or shoal, around them, are a group of nine small islands off the Maine and New Hampshire coasts. Many forms of wildlife live on these rockbound islands, which are constantly battered by the Atlantic Ocean.

J Blue jays are common throughout the woodlands of New Hampshire. Their loud screams will wake you early in the morning.

K This kitten is playing in a camper's knapsack. New Hampshire is a favorite place for campers and hikers.

L The lilac is New Hampshire's state flower.

M Old Man of the Mountain in Franconia Notch is a rock formation that took shape over 200 million years ago. The Old Man's "profile" is composed of five separate granite ledges and measures almost forty feet high.

N There are many natural notches (passes between two mountains) in New Hampshire. Dixville Notch is in the northern wilderness region of the state, where there are also scenic gorges, waterfalls, and beautiful unspoiled terrain.

O These barred owls are waiting until nightfall to hunt for food. The owls' large eyes help them hunt at night, as they fly noiselessly through the woods.

P This view of Portsmouth Harbor shows the city skyline and the powerful tugs used to push large vessels in and out of the port.

Q These quilters are representative of the many craftspeople in New Hampshire. Small "cottage industries" are an important part of the state's economy.

R The masked raccoons are a delightful combination of rogue and clown. They will eat almost anything and often will noisily raid garbage cans late at night.

S New Hampshire's coastline is only a few miles long. Sandy beaches cover much of that distance.

T New Hampshire has much to offer the sport fisherman. Saltwater fish are plentiful near the coast, and freshwater fish such as trout, salmon, and bass can be caught in the lakes and streams.

U In the rocks of the Granite State are many minerals such as feldspar, quartz, tourmaline, and pyrite. At the Ruggles Mine, mica was produced as early as 1803 for use in lamp chimneys and stove windows.

V Each region of New Hampshire has its own beauty. This is the scenic Connecticut Valley.

W Mount Washington is the highest mountain in the northeast, standing 6,288 feet above sea level. It is unusually windy at the summit. In 1934, the wind velocity reached 232 miles per hour, the highest speed ever recorded anywhere in the world.

X New Hampshire has many lakes, and Winnipesaukee is the largest. Swimming, sailing, and water skiing are popular summer lake sports. These water skiers are making extra-large (XL) X-shaped patterns with their ropes and the wakes of their skis.

Y This Yankee lad is enjoying the Fourth of July with two of his friends.

Z From early spring wild flowers to late fall foliage, New Hampshire displays an endless variety of colors. Zinnias bloom in midsummer. *Can you find the butterfly?*